the

CHRISTMAS STONE

LIZ CARLSTON

the CHRISTMAS STONE

LIZ CARLSTON

Bonneville Books
Springville, Utah

This is a work of fiction. The characters, names, incidents, places, and dialogue are products of the author's imagination, and are not to be construed as real.

ISBN 13: 978-1-59955-434-1

Published by Bonneville Books, an imprint of Cedar Fort, Inc., 2373 W. 700 S., Springville, UT 84663
Distributed by Cedar Fort, Inc. www.cedarfort.com

LIBRARY OF CONGRESS CATALOGING-IN-PUBLICATION DATA

Carlston, Liz.
  The Christmas Stone / Liz Carlston.
    p. cm.
  ISBN 978-1-59955-434-1 (acid-free paper)
  1. Holiday compassion--Fiction. 2. Neighbors--Fiction. I.
Title.

  PS3603.A7536C48 2010
  813'.6--dc22

            2010013384

Cover design by Tanya Quinlan
Cover design © 2010 by Lyle Mortimer
Edited and typeset by Heidi Doxey

Printed in the United States of America

10 9 8 7 6 5 4 3 2 1

Printed on acid-free paper

Almost everyone has a stone to throw. Some stones turn into second chances . . .

one

Claire gasped for air. Her stiletto heels clicked loudly as she descended a short flight of stairs, pushing past two coworkers standing in the hallway near the front lobby.

"Hey, Claire, it's about time you took a vacation," the receptionist called out from behind the front desk as Claire hurried past. Refusing to acknowledge her, Claire rushed to the freedom beyond the heavy glass-paneled doors.

In a frazzled dash to her car, she reached into her purse, searching for keys. She quickly unlocked the silver Mercedes' door, settled into the seat, and peeled out of the parking lot. Once situated, she stared out the window through blurry tear-filled eyes.

Her father sure had horrible timing. The night before, Claire's cell phone had woken her unexpectedly.

Groggily reaching to turn on her bedside lamp, Claire grabbed for the phone. It was her mother.

"Honey, I'm so sorry to be calling you this late, but your dad is in the hospital. They're doing more tests in the morning, but the preliminary CT scan makes them suspect a tumor. I need you to come home."

"This really isn't convenient, but I guess this kind of thing never is," Claire grumbled. "I'll catch tomorrow's first flight to Milwaukee."

She pulled herself out of bed and made an early afternoon reservation on the laptop she kept on her bed-side desk. After she clicked the confirmation button, she rubbed her eyes and glanced up at the screen's calendar bar. December 23rd.

"It's about time I made it home for the holidays," she murmured to herself.

Before the phone call, she had bought gifts to show she remembered her parents. The KitchenAid mixer for her mother should have arrived weeks earlier, along with a new leather recliner for her father since the footrest on his chair hadn't worked properly in years.

In the morning, Claire had packed quickly. She even tried squeezing in a few hours of work before her flight, but the stress of unexpectedly leaving her team coupled with her father's illness was too much to handle.

Now speeding down the highway, she loosened her iron-clad grip on the steering wheel and breathed in deeply. Competing thoughts exploded in her mind before one settled. *Be still.* Knowing she had to calm down, Claire changed course, taking an exit that led toward Lookout Mountain.

Gravel crunched under the tires as her car finally came to a halt off the paved road. Cool mountain air chilled her face as she opened the door. She slipped on the pair of comfortable shoes she always kept on the passenger seat and stepped out onto an overlook. Her slender frame moved with ease as her feet stepped carefully to avoid patches of ice and packed mud.

Staring down at the frozen lake that stretched toward a snow-covered precipice on the other end of the gorge, she took a cautious step back. On the ridge where she was perched, a breeze stirred the loose strands of her long auburn hair, creating a soft whisper of sound.

She glanced at her Blackberry and was disappointed to see there were no bars displayed on the screen. The sensation of being disconnected from her office was always unsettling since she couldn't respond to emails from clients or co-workers.

Claire's job forced her to pull long hours, but she hedged exhaustion through jolts of caffeine. Her office wastebasket was always filled with crushed Dr. Pepper cans. As long as a stroke didn't kill her first, Claire was counting on the hard work to earn her a seat at the executive's table. But today, following a muddy trail up the steep hillside, Claire worried she was having a nervous breakdown.

She had taken easily to the lifestyle her six-figure salary with a leading bio-technology company afforded her. A car dealer had had little trouble convincing her to trade in a used clunker for a sleek sports car. She lived in a luxury condo, and friends came easily—as long as Claire picked up the check. Given her compulsive drive to succeed at work, she was far more likely to spend the night with a movie rental than with a guy.

As clouds drifted by in the blue sky overhead, a blistering wind shot across the hill, bringing Claire's thoughts back to the mountain scene sprawled before her. Her short hike had brought her halfway up a foothill of the rugged Rocky Mountains, which loomed high above her. She paused in her uphill climb, breathed in the clean air, and thought about her life.

In spite of her financial success and the way her career was going, she wasn't entirely happy. Claire knew things weren't as they should be and was dealing daily with a familiar ache that seemed to lessen up here. Chills raced up her spine, and she folded her arms to warm her body.

"What am I supposed to do now?" she whispered to the valley.

A growing void expanded inside her chest. She had no brothers and sisters, no close friends to share her grief. She had left the empty space in her life undisturbed for far too long. Her unrealistic expectations and drive for perfection controlled her. But these things didn't give hugs or comfort. Instead, like leeches, they sucked the life and meaning from her soulless world.

The people she so desperately tried to

impress with her work ethic didn't care. They all had families to take care of, kids' soccer games to attend, and neighborhood barbecues to host. Unlike Claire, they had lives away from the office.

Looking at her watch, Claire realized she was out of time and had to get to the airport. She began the trek back down the hill toward her car. After belting herself into the seat and starting the powerful engine, a jumble of emotions washed over her.

She hated that her dad was sick. And she felt guilty for having distanced herself from the only people who truly loved her. She needed to help her parents, but she was as powerless to stop her father's illness as she was to heal the emptiness of her own soul.

Fighting the ache gnawing at her, she thought if she could just get to her father's bedside, everything would be all right. The thought gave her strength. Pulling the car into gear, she cruised down the mountain switchbacks with tears muddying her vision. Claire had a plane to catch.

two

Looking into his bag of sorted mail, the postman grabbed several envelopes and dropped them into the slotted door of a two-story home in an upscale Milwaukee neighborhood. He strolled away as Anne picked up the pile inside her doorway. Nearly fumbling the bills and advertisements, she scrutinized the crisp white envelope with the California return address. She recognized the city name, and memories—most of them painful—flooded into her mind.

Why, after so many years, was he doing this to her? She had buried him. Shuffling back down the polished oak hallway, she heard Bryce call from the study.

"Did you get the mail, sweetie?"

Anne met his gaze as she entered the room.

"You look pale. What's wrong?" Bryce asked, standing up from his seat behind a maplewood desk. She walked over to him and sat down heavily in his chair. Picking up the letter opener from the corner of the desk, she tore open the envelope. The force of the action startled her, and she quickly dropped both items on the desk. Bryce glanced at the return address and then lifted his stare to her troubled brown eyes.

"Would you like me to read it first?" he asked.

Anne painfully nodded a yes as he pulled out three hand-written sheets of paper.

December 6

Dear Anne,

I know this is unexpected, and it must be difficult for you to read. I've been a coward and held onto my pride for too long. Walking out on you was the biggest mistake of my life. I punish myself every day for leaving.

Remember our first Christmas together? Beside the fireplace with our tiny tree, you put a love letter in my stocking and I kissed your cheek. Your goodness is one thing I can never forget.

Watching Spencer grow up and seeing his willingness to extend forgiveness for my mistakes was a result of your generous heart. I am not worthy of your forgiveness, but I feel I need to see you and make things as right as possible.

All those years ago, when I heard you had remarried, I was thrilled for you. I wasn't as fortunate and I didn't deserve to be. I should have cherished you and defended our family. Nothing should have ever destroyed it, and I am sincerely sorry. My guilt is a burden, a stone that I've carried for twenty-five years. But it's time to let it go.

Please agree to see me. I don't expect anything to change between us, but I need your forgiveness for my healing to be complete. After a layover in Denver, my flight arrives in Milwaukee the day before Christmas Eve. I want to apologize face-to-face. Will you please meet me at the airport?

Yours,

Daniel

"He wants to apologize in person for being a jerk," Bryce said flatly. "And he wants you to pick him up at the airport. This joker can get a cab. Leave him waiting on the curb like he left you!"

Anne could no longer hold back tears. Like a tidal wave, years of hurt quickly rushed over her as she remembered Daniel's betrayal and abandonment. Facing those people at church alone with Spencer after Daniel walked out had been too difficult. She'd spent countless nights wondering why she hadn't been pretty enough or smart enough to keep him, wondering what she had done wrong.

Letting Daniel's letter fall from his hands, Bryce wrapped his arms around Anne and held her close. "You really don't owe him a thing," he whispered. "I don't want him to hurt you again."

She cried silently for a few moments before pulling away from her husband. "I think I need to meet him," she said, setting aside her anger and pain. "He needs this. He didn't have someone as good as you to help him move on, like I did." Silence filled the room but was immediately broken by Anne's laugh. "Remember when we met?"

Bryce chuckled, "Yeah, I held twenty dollars ransom, making you get out of your car to come see me in the bank. I probably could have been fired, but it eventually turned out in my favor."

"I was so scared of starting over," she said distantly. "Thank you for loving me and Spencer. You've helped make Daniel's deceit a distant memory." She gazed sadly at the letter sitting on the desk. "But now . . ."

three

As the 737 from Los Angeles came to a halt in front of gate A-34 at Denver International Airport, passengers unfastened their seat belts and scurried to collect their belongings from the overhead bins. After two hours of tight confinement, as if it was a race, they anxiously scrambled to leave the tubular prison.

Welcoming the chance to exit the plane while it was being prepped for its continuing flight, Daniel walked past a smiling flight attendant and captain toward the freedom of the cabin door. Thoughts of a hot drink from Starbucks filled his mind, especially as he looked out the terminal's ten-foot-high windows to see the snowstorm that greeted him.

Marching with a group of travel-weary passengers, Daniel approached the barista counter and took his place at the back of the line. His hope that Anne would in fact meet him and hear him out was interrupted by the hiss of the cappuccino machine.

Just two more hours and I'll be flying to Milwaukee, Daniel thought to himself. *Then this nightmare will all be a distant memory.*

After taking his money and spraying a layer of whipped cream on his drink, the barista handed Daniel his cup and pastry. He thanked the server and made his way to the gate. Each passing step seemed to augment his growing anticipation. He was nervous but also eager to have closure. Daniel felt certain that after his conversation with Anne the demon that had plagued him since he walked out on her would finally leave.

Truly he had never intended to hurt Anne, but the excitement of living a double life was too tempting. To him, getting everything he wanted came with the territory of success. Sometimes people got hurt. A lot of the guys at the studio had affairs—it wasn't a big deal. Besides, at the time he had reasoned that since he was the one who provided a big home and put food on the table, Anne and Spencer should have been grateful, no matter what he did. But now he realized he was the real loser.

At the departure gate, Daniel took his pick from dozens of vacant blue vinyl chairs lining the waiting area. Laying his heavy coat across a neighboring chair, Daniel sat down and rested the pastry on his jean-covered knee.

Thinking of his son, Daniel smiled as he recalled a three-day scout trip they took together. A bony little kid, Spencer was anxious to prove his strength on the lake.

"Let's try the canoe, Dad! I wanna see how fast we can paddle."

Dipping his oar into the water, Spencer pulled back as hard as his little arms could move. While Daniel got settled in the back, Spencer stood, trying to improve his angle. The awkward position caused the canoe to tip. Eventually, Daniel broke the surface with water dripping down his face. Spencer greeted him eagerly with a wide toothy grin. "That was fun! Can we try it again?"

Daniel chuckled to himself. *He's a good kid.* He took a tentative sip from his cup and paused as the PA system turned on.

"Due to blizzard conditions, Flight 1297 to Milwaukee will be delayed," a female airline representative spoke over the intercom. "We apologize for the inconvenience and will keep you posted as the weather improves."

Groans from unhappy passengers swept across the terminal as other flight delays were also announced.

"Oh, come on, how long will that take?" Daniel grumbled. He had hoped to make it a quick trip and wanted to get to Milwaukee to be with his son for Christmas. Turning his head to stare at the storm outside, he pulled out his cell phone and dialed Spencer's number. Spencer's phone must have been turned off because the call went straight to voicemail.

"Hi, Spence! Hey, my plane is delayed so I'll be getting in a little late. Will you let your mom know? I'll call you when I land. I love you, son. Good-bye."

four

The snowstorm swept in quickly from the west, leaving a slick layer of ice on the roads. By keeping an eye out for shiny black pools on the road, Claire was able to maneuver her vehicle around the ice without much difficulty. The weather was typical for Colorado. Claire cautiously steered her car into the covered, long-term airport parking lot and, with her charcoal Samsonite luggage in tow, hurried past the automatic glass doors to check in.

Dodging clumps of holiday travelers, Claire was relieved to see that her flight to Milwaukee was delayed. She went to the restroom to change into more comfortable clothes. After hanging her coat on the stall door, she put on a wool sweater and jeans and replaced the pair of trendy slip-on shoes on her feet. Stuffing her red blouse and black slacks into her carry-on, Claire grabbed her coat and left the bathroom.

Proud of her ability to breeze through security, Claire rode the crowded shuttle train to her terminal. Squeezed between a large man and a woman's carry-on, Claire tried focusing on her father. His illness revealed the ugly truth about the fragility of life. It was an unfortunate reminder to reassess her priorities and remember what mattered most in life—her family and friends.

Not knowing where to start, Claire offered a silent prayer. Maybe there was a little Christmas magic in the air. After all, the holiday was just around the corner. At times like these, her mind reached back to a church lesson from her youth.

The teacher taught that just as a child takes broken toys to his parents, expecting them to be mended, we bring our challenges to God, wanting them fixed. Growing impatient, we often snatch them back, angry they're still broken. As we blame God, He says, "How can I fix them if you never let go?"

Perhaps that was the reason Claire was praying now. She was letting go. Her isolation and guilt were melting away. It was as though a voice had whispered in her ear that life would be changing for the better very soon.

"Good thing that ice storm cleared out—I guess it wouldn't be Christmas without the snow," the air traffic controller said to his colleague while sipping from a hot mug. The fast-moving storm had passed quickly, and they could once again grant pilots permission to take off. But first, the planes had to be de-iced.

Below the tower, huge cranes that looked like cherry pickers were circling the planes. Workers in yellow firefighterlike suits and masks straddled pressure hoses to blast the planes with antifreeze.

Standing on a truck's hydraulic platform, overlooking a plane's wing, a new worker shivered. His partner climbed onto the wing and pulled off his glove. Scratching the surface, he inspected his fingernails for frost. He didn't use high-tech tools, just his eyes and hands.

"We gotta get this stuff off the fuselage and wings too," he said. "See, it's fluffy snow, but there's still frost on the surface. We can't let anything go if there's ice on it."

He evaluated another plane that had just passed through the decontamination process. The plane was clear. All 160 passengers could now catch their Wisconsin flight.

"Last boarding call for Milwaukee," the PA system crackled.

Lost in her thoughts and thinking she had more time to wait, Claire had somehow missed the other boarding announcements. Now, suddenly aware that she was late and juggling a purse, coat, and carry-on bag, Claire sprinted toward the gate. She looked around the empty waiting area and ran faster.

"You barely made it," the middle-aged desk clerk said, scanning the end of her boarding pass. "Merry Christmas."

"You too, thanks," Claire mumbled as she darted

into the jetway. As she sheepishly entered the cabin door, all eyes stared at her. She apologetically made her way down the aisle toward her seat.

Oh, no, she thought. Her window-seat, 9A, was next to a grey-haired gentleman who was smiling affably. He looked to be about fifty years old, and though he was nicely dressed and his blue eyes exhibited warmth and friendliness, she wasn't looking to make a new friend. *This will be a long flight.*

"I guess this is my seat," Claire said to him.

"How about that!" he exclaimed. "I love when they put me next to the pretty girls!" Claire's face flashed an insincere smile as she groaned inaudibly.

The man stood to let Claire pass, and after they had both stowed their things and buckled their seat belts, he turned to introduce himself as Daniel.

"I'm Claire," she said. "Are you going home for Christmas?"

"Not exactly. I'm from Los Angeles but I'm going to visit my son and his mom," Daniel replied. "How about you? Are you on your way home to visit family?"

She was determined not to engage him in a long conversation, but to her surprise the details quickly poured out about her father's condition and prospective outlook.

"I haven't been home in a long time, and with my dad's illness, Mom says this may be the last time I'll see him," Claire said soberly. "They've always been my anchor. If anything happens to Dad, I'm not sure what I'll do."

"You're a good daughter to go home to be with them," Daniel said, smiling reassuringly. "It's not an easy thing going back after a lot of time has passed, but I'm sure there'll be lots of hugs and happiness when you get there."

Claire sat quietly, trying to envision the scene Daniel had painted. She smiled at the thought of being together with her parents, but still her guilt lingered. As the flight attendant's voice buzzed over the intercom, explaining the emergency procedures, Claire turned to Daniel and asked about his son.

"My wife and I divorced when Spencer was just a little boy," Daniel began. "He visited me every summer and every other Christmas in California. At the moment, he works as an architect, designing new buildings in Wisconsin. I couldn't be more proud of him."

Daniel fumbled in his wallet before pulling out a picture of Spencer standing next to an older woman, who Claire assumed was Spencer's mother. The young man was handsome with blue eyes, like his dad, and he wore his sandy blond hair cut short. Spencer's mother had retained a youthful appearance, lacking grey hair or wrinkles. Standing a few inches shorter than her son, she seemed poised and confident with her arm around Spencer's waist.

"He's good-looking, don't you think?" Daniel said, winking. Politely, she nodded back to him.

Outside the cabin, the engines roared, and the plane picked up speed, hurtling down the runway for longer than seemed necessary before the wheels finally lifted off the ground, and they were airborne. After gaining altitude, the plane leveled and the engines quieted to a soothing hum. The cabin's changing pressure made Claire yawn as she tried to pop her ears.

"If you don't mind my asking, why did you divorce?" Claire inquired.

Daniel grimaced and shook his head before

responding. "I was young and extremely stupid."

Unsatisfied with his answer, Claire probed, "When was the last time all three of you were together?"

"Would you care for anything to drink?" a flight attendant asked, taking orders on a square notepad. Looking relieved by the interruption, Daniel said, "Cranberry juice, please."

"And for you?" she asked Claire.

"I'll have a Dr. Pepper, please," Claire answered.

"Is Mr. Pibb all right?" the attendant asked.

"Sure," Claire conceded.

Daniel didn't immediately respond to Claire's question. Instead he made small talk about how flying was no longer the sophisticated adventure it used to be. "I remember when they served wonderful meals and everyone dressed up to fly. Now it's more like being on a bus in the sky."

It wasn't until the attendant delivered their drinks that Daniel finally responded to Claire's question. His voice failed him a bit as he said, "Pride is poison. I blamed everyone but myself— that's what has taken so long. I had to take a long hard look at myself and push through my fears to do the right thing. I guess I've finally concluded that it's a chapter in my life I haven't properly closed. I need to apologize."

Not knowing quite how to respond, Claire waited for him to go on.

"Cocktail parties, celebrity friends, and female coworkers were part of my Hollywood lawyer lifestyle. I remember one night Spencer was sick with a fever, and Anne called my office. My secretary picked up the phone. I can still hear that conversation in my head."

"This is very urgent. I need to speak with Daniel. Spencer is sick," Anne said.

"Umm, he's tied up at the moment," Heather giggled. "Can I take your message?"

"I expected him home hours ago." Anne spoke more boldly than usual. "This is his wife, and I need to speak with him now."

A long pause cut the conversation before Heather agreed to deliver the message.

"I never returned the call." He spoke just above a whisper. "I came home late, after Anne had taken Spencer to the doctor, filled his prescription, and put him to bed."

Glancing out the window while processing his words, Claire saw a frozen cobalt Midwestern sky. Lines of wet tearlike snow streaked across the Plexiglas, pushed back by the plane's thrust. They'd been in the air over an hour before Daniel reached into his pocket and took out a small stone. An inch round in size, the flat stone was crimson colored, smooth on top, and rough on the bottom.

"Have you ever seen a magic rock before?" Daniel asked, smiling mischievously. Claire raised an eyebrow and shook her head. At a glance, the rock was inanimate. Claire knew that some people believed stones had healing powers, but the object in Daniel's hand was all too ordinary.

"You could say it's been a crutch, but for me this rock represents a choice, a second chance," he said. "Letting people in and taking chances is life's secret if you ask me."

Claire considered Daniel's statement. It had taken her the better part of her lifetime to let anyone in. All too often, work was an easy distraction. Without it, Claire's mind constantly filled with thoughts of inadequacy that controlled her mood and attitude. Besides her parents, her grandma was the only person Claire had ever felt truly connected with.

As a self-conscious seven-year-old, Claire's face had been sprinkled with bright freckles, and she was the tallest in her class.

"You're like a giant giraffe!" a boy teased. Others joined in laughing as a humiliated Claire dropped her head.

Later in the day, as Claire walked home, she found her grandma waiting for her. Grandma's visits were frequent since she lived only a few miles away, and Claire was especially grateful for her today. With a broken heart, Claire told her grandma about the boy and how he had compared her to a giraffe.

"When I was a little girl, I always wanted to be tall," Grandma said, tracing her finger across the child's cheek. "Your height is beautiful."

Claire looked up. "Really?"

"Of course," said her grandma. "Why, just name me one thing that's prettier than a tall, lovely girl."

Thinking for a moment, Claire peered intensely into her grandma's face and softly whispered, "Wrinkles." Smiling, her grandma wrapped Claire in a warm hug and invited her inside to enjoy an ice cream sandwich.

That was one of the last memories Claire had with her grandma.

When her grandma had died a short time later, Claire felt as though her own ability to connect with others had also died.

"I guess it's important to focus on the lessons life teaches us, rather than the things we've lost," Claire said to Daniel.

He took a deep breath before responding, "I wish life came with a guidebook. Inside all of us, I believe there's a simple force helping us to be better and leading us to build people. When we do, it builds us, in turn."

He glanced at his gold Rolex. Only thirty more minutes until he'd be with Spencer and Anne. He'd finally be able to move forward and not hurt anymore. Turning to Claire, he asked if she was dating anyone.

"No, my job keeps me pretty busy," she answered.

After pausing a moment, he said, "If you wanted, I'd be happy to set you up with Spencer. Since you'll be out here for a few weeks, it might do both of you some good to have a little fun."

"Oh, . . . I don't know . . ." she began. Meeting some stranger was the last thing she wanted to do.

"Come on," Daniel coaxed. "He's a terrific

kid. Just go out and have some laughs together. What could it hurt?" He had his pen out and was writing.

She felt trapped but didn't want to offend this nice man. Thinking she would simply throw it away later, she accepted the cocktail napkin with Spencer's name and phone number scrawled in blue ink.

five

Rolling the stone between his thumb and fingers, Daniel grinned as he remembered discovering the rock. Wishing to share the memory, he turned toward Claire. She appeared lost in her own thoughts, and he hesitated before speaking.

"You know, I found this stone almost fifteen years ago," he began. "I found it the same day I bought a new cherry-red Corvette.

"I was heading home through the neighborhood and hardly noticed the boy standing on a grassy lawn a few yards up the road. As I passed him, something hard smashed into my side door. I slammed on the brakes and jumped out, furious that my new car had been hit. I ran toward the boy, yelling, 'What did you do that for? This is a new car!'

"The boy was really apologetic. He was scared and mumbled, 'I nee-needed your help because nobody stopped.' Then the boy gasped for breath before continuing. "I tri-tried to hit your tire.'

"With tears dripping off his chin, the boy pointed toward a tree with a body writhing around on the ground.

"'It's my brother,' the kid whimpered. 'He fell and hu-hurt his leg. I can't lift him, and no one came to help me.'

"Forgetting my car, I dialed 911 and ran over to the younger boy, who was holding his leg in pain beneath the tree. While we were waiting for the ambulance, I calmed his brother down long enough for him to give me their mom's phone number. She got there just as the paramedics arrived. They gave him a quick look-over and said the boy's leg was broken, but that he would be okay.

"I don't know why, but the accident really shook me up. I watched the family leave for the hospital and then headed back to my Corvette. The damage to my car was very noticeable, but I never bothered to repair the dent. I picked this rock up from the gutter, the same rock that desperate boy had thrown."

He held it out for Claire to see in the palm of his hand. "I suppose I could have sent the kid's mom a bill for my car's damages, but the right thing happened in the end. I've kept it ever since because it reminds me that the people we love—our family—matter more than the things we have or achieve."

Balancing the stone in the palm of his hand, he continued, "Anne had taken Spencer and left me by then, and I began thinking about what I was missing. She was a wonderful person, and my other relationships were empty and meaning-less. I couldn't open my heart to another decent woman because I was afraid I would hurt her like I'd hurt Anne. Holding this stone, I began to realize for the first time that I could forgive myself and let the healing process begin."

Claire listened somewhat uneasily to this candid confession. She had only just met Daniel. Uncomfortably, she considered why Daniel was even on this airplane. In a quick turn of thought, she wondered if the stone really did have magic powers. Then another reflection came—maybe he was just crazy.

six

The muffled whine of the 737's wing flaps changed in pitch, signaling the plane's descent to Milwaukee. Through the window, Claire could see snowflakes streaking through the plane's bright spotlights and ice accumulating on the wing. A slight tremor rocked the fuselage as the captain's voice sounded over the intercom, informing the passengers that they were on a glide path to the airport and asking them to fasten their seat belts. He reported they would experience a little turbulence as they descended, but assured them everything was under control.

The plane bounced and shuddered, causing Claire to grip her arm rests with white knuckles. A few passengers behind her laughed nervously as they experienced the momentary weightlessness. Then the captain's voice was heard again, this time sounding a lot more serious.

"Ladies and gentlemen, please keep your seat belts fastened. We have ice building up on the wings, and it's making the plane fly heavy. And with the cold temperatures outside, we've got some cause for concern. But we'll just have to ride it out. I apologize for the bumps. We should be on the ground in a few short minutes."

The intercom shut off, and Claire felt the tension rise inside the cabin in the dreadful silence.

She should have seen a glowing urban grid and city lights outside the window, but instead she saw only a blanket of white. The delay in Denver had set them back hours into the night. And she knew that the freezing temperatures and humidity made conditions ripe for ice to collect on the wings and pass through the engines.

Suddenly the plane's balance disappeared, and, in a free fall, the engines momentarily flamed out. A look through the windows offered only an ominous white-out. Then the plane jerked down, which she knew was an emergency maneuver pilots used to avoid an aerodynamic stall.

Claire heard several passengers scream while she glanced over to see others tucking their heads between their knees. Several prayed repetitiously, "Lord, forgive me for my sins."

Daniel's jaw tightened, and he returned the stone to his pocket. Claire quickly glanced behind her to review where the exit rows were. She saw a broad-shouldered man sitting by the exit door reading the safety card.

Across the aisle, a woman's fingers scrambled out a text message on her cell phone. Then the woman tilted her head back, dropped the phone, and stared at the ceiling as tears dripped down her cheek. Claire hoped it wouldn't be the woman's final farewell to a loved one.

Speedily, the flight attendants took charge. "There are three bracing positions," an attendant frantically yelled from the front of the aircraft. "Head forward, hands over your head, and feet firmly planted behind your knees so they won't shoot forward on impact."

Another ominous warning came from the captain: "We're going down. Brace for impact."

Sheer terror engulfed the passengers as they tried to secure their bodies against seat backs and the overhead compartment to prevent the impact of the inevitable g-force. Many were speaking on their cell phones, offering good-byes to loved ones. From the rear, a flight attendant was shouting, "Brace, brace! Heads down! Stay down!"

Daniel felt like he was in a nightmare, the kind where the ground breaks out from under your feet and you fall with nothing to grab onto. He shook his head and breathed in to clear his mind. As the plane descended, he decided to make sure women and children got out first. Then he reached over and took Claire's hand in his.

With two crippled engines, the pilot guided the plane toward a glasslike body of water. The blizzard had buffeted the plane from the left side, knocking it off course by more than two miles. Given the limited visibility, Lake Michigan was the only forgiving place the pilot could think of to land the aircraft. With its nose up, the jetliner glided as the tail hit the water first with a hard thud. Luggage, coats, and bags plummeted violently out of the overhead bins as people screamed.

Then the front of the plane slammed belly-down on the lake and a volcano of water shot up outside the windows, rippling in the distance.

As if in a rear-end collision, Daniel and the other passengers were thrown into the seats ahead of them. Everyone seemed to wait for someone else to shout in pain, and for a time, no one spoke. The passengers sat stunned and silent.

As soon as the plane settled on the water, Claire watched a flight attendant nearest the cockpit remove her seat belt and bolt toward the door, pushing passengers aside. She pulled the handle to remove the hatch, triggering an automatic chute to deploy. As the balloon inflated, the life raft shot out, creating a makeshift floating walkway. Because the water was still below the aircraft door, this sequence of emergency procedures went off without a hitch.

She came back from the door and faced the cabin. "Please remain calm. We must evacuate the aircraft safely. No pushing or shoving. Be sure to put your life vests on. Remember, they are under your seat, but don't inflate them until you're outside!"

Claire heard a man seated in the emergency row lecture the woman next to him, struggling with the latch. She tried pulling the door in. "No," he said, "you've got to push it out." He reached across her and, twisting the knob, threw the hatch away from the plane.

As passengers disembarked, Claire stood alongside Daniel. They looked toward the cockpit and saw the captain and co-pilot work their communication equipment to send out distress signals, requesting immediate aid from the Coast Guard. The temperature outside was below freezing, and as soon as everyone's adrenaline ran out, it would get very cold.

seven

Standing outside on the wing, a woman wearing a fur coat asked a stranger to go back inside the slowly sinking plane to fetch her purse. As snow fell across his face, the man laughed at her, saying no one would be going back inside. She huffed away from him in anger, passing a young man who tenderly kissed his fiancée. The winds began picking up, and the couple struggled to maintain their footing on the wing's slick and moving surface. Everyone waited helplessly for rescue boats to arrive as they watched the choppy water beat into the side of the plane.

Inside the cabin a mother clutched her infant son to her chest as she scrambled over seats to avoid the stampede. A hysterical woman suddenly screamed, "We're going to die!" and a new level of chaos erupted in the cabin. People pushed their way into the aisle and began shoving toward the emergency exits.

Daniel shouted, "Keep calm! We'll get out of here, but only if we help each other." His words fell on deaf ears as full-blown panic set in.

Five rows behind him, Daniel saw a middle-aged woman tussling with a teenager. Reaching for her carry-on, she blocked the aisle as the teen yelled at her, "Leave it! Just get out of here!" Refusing, she screamed back, "I'm taking my stuff!" A balding man with wire-rimmed glasses put his arms around her waist from behind and picked her up, hauling her forcibly to the door where he threw her outside and onto a lifeboat chute. The bag she'd held in her hand now floated aimlessly on the lake. The same man turned and yelled back at everyone else, "We need to get out *now*!"

The odor of burning electronics and a smoky haze began filling the plane. The cabin lights flickered and then went off, bathing the frantic scene in only a dim yellow light from the emergency globes lining the floor of the fuselage. As the huge plane settled further into the cold lake, people felt their shoes and socks absorb the bone-chilling moisture. Many of the passengers near the front of the cabin had already escaped. But Claire spotted an elderly woman a few rows away still sitting in her seat. She went to the woman, only to find her crying in pain and worry.

"You need to get out!" Claire said frantically.

"It hurts to move. I'm afraid I have injured my leg, and I can't breathe," the woman replied.

"Daniel!" Claire shouted over the chaos and noise. "I need your help."

After assisting another disabled passenger out the door, Daniel hurried back to help Claire. He freed the fragile woman from her seat belt and then reached down to gently pick her up. "This is going to hurt, but we need to get you out of here." She murmured with pain as he carefully navigated her down the aisle and passed her through the open door into the arms of a waiting crew member, cautious not to let the woman's head hit the doorway.

"Claire, you have to get out of here too," Daniel said, turning to look her in the eyes. "I'm going to keep helping the others, and I'll meet up with you outside. Here," he said, handing her the little stone. "Don't lose this—it means a lot to me."

Clutching her purse, Claire quickly moved to the nearest exit and jumped out the opening onto one of the floating emergency slides.

Daniel glanced toward the back of the airplane. He could see water shooting through cracks in the wall, quickly pouring into the cabin. The back of the plane was slowly sinking and was now submerged in the icy water up to the cabin windows. Daniel could see a fellow passenger throwing flotation devices out the doors to people gathered on the wings. He joined the man.

Looking outside, Daniel was relieved to see the flood lights of rescue boats beginning to arrive and starting to collect the wet and cold passengers.

eight

Horrified, Mercado watched the plane smack down with a crash that rattled his teeth and nerves.

His seven-year-old ferry, built in Wisconsin, was a nimble four-diesel engine vessel, and it looked like they would be the first to reach the plane. He quickly changed course toward the aircraft as the radio squawked with news of the event. The Coast Guard would arrive soon, but for now, he needed to get to that plane.

As they neared the airliner, Mercado could see that it was drifting south on the steady three-knot current—with people crowded on the wings and some in the water, clinging to flotation devices. They would need to get to the plane quickly before it drifted further away.

"It's an every-man-for-himself rescue!" Mercado yelled to his crew.

As he drew the ferry alongside one of the inflatable chutes, he saw more than forty people huddled together, cold, half-naked, and screaming in terror. Others were standing waist-deep in water on the submerged wings. Some were treading water in the lake. News helicopters were hovering low. Their blades whipped up the water, spraying the passengers below.

A drenched flight attendant had been fished out of the frigid water and was suffering from hypothermia. One man, thinking he would have to swim, had stripped on the plane and was wearing only boxer shorts as he was hauled aboard the ferry. Another man slipped from the wing into the water, but members of the crew soon pulled him onto the ferry. Wrapped in a blanket, he curled into the fetal position, freezing.

One by one, Mercado's crew pulled up passengers. In less than twelve minutes following splashdown, Mercado's crew had pulled forty-three people aboard. Some were bleeding. All were wet and shivering. The crew wrapped people in emergency blankets and shared their dry coats. They used first-aid kits to treat head, arm, and leg abrasions

Then Mercado saw a couple with young children slowly make their way onto the wing. They were very cautious, holding tight to their kids, including a baby in its mother's arms. In an effort to help, others grabbed the children away. The mother stood on the wing, crying hysterically.

Women on the ferry screamed out, "Give us the baby—throw us the baby!" but the mother wouldn't do it. Eventually, two male passengers intervened. One grabbed the mother and the other her baby and heaved them up to waiting hands.

"Where's my baby?" the woman continued to scream. Another lady handed over the infant. "No, I mean my two-year-old!" No one could answer.

The water was now rising even faster in the cabin. For the past several minutes, Daniel and his partner had been working together, moving

injured people from the plane.

Daniel quickly looked forward and aft in the near darkness, checking to see who might remain in the cabin.

"I think we got everyone," the man yelled from the rear, where water now covered the seat backs of rows 22 through 26. Standing in row 12, near the exit, Daniel watched water gushing through the door.

"Let's get out of here!" he called to the man who was searching the opposite end of the cabin for survivors.

The inflated emergency slides at the rear and center of the fuselage had already detached to avoid being sucked down by the sinking plane. Wading up the aisle in waist-deep water toward the cockpit where he knew life rafts were still attached, Daniel heard a muffled cry coming from row 4. He paused and found a young boy still buckled into his seat belt, cowering next to the window, with water rising to just below his chin.

Instantly, Daniel's mind shot back twenty-five years, to the night before he left Anne and his two-year-old Spencer.

Coming home late from the office once again,

*he'd decided to check on his son. He found Spencer,
contentedly smiling in his sleep, hugging a soft teddy
bear. So innocent, so pure. Daniel would have given
his life for Spencer. He would have done anything to
protect him.*

Daniel quickly unsnapped the seat belt and
tried to lift the boy, but the little body wouldn't
move. His leg was wedged beneath the seat back
of a chair that had shifted position in the crash.

"Help me!" Daniel yelled to his partner, while
trying to free the boy's leg. The boy's skin was
blue, his body cold, and his breathing labored.
The other man held the boy securely, prepared to
drag him away as Daniel lifted the seat off him.

"On three, okay? One, two, three!"

Grunting from the weight of the chair, Daniel
lifted it just far enough to free the boy's leg. However, the water surging into the cabin acted as
a catalyst to bring a neighboring seat down on
Daniel's foot and hand. He was pinned, and the
water level was only a few inches from his face.
Holding the boy in his arms, Daniel's partner
stopped to help.

"Go! Save yourself and the boy. I'll figure a
way out," Daniel said.

The man was torn, his eyes wide with fear as he tried to decide how he could save the boy and help Daniel.

"There's no more time!" Daniel yelled. "Save him!" The man turned and waded toward the front of the plane, holding the boy's body up and out of the water.

Stretching his neck as high as he could, Daniel sucked in one last gulp of air before water covered his face.

nine

Anne was a little early in her drive to meet Daniel at the airport. Instead of circling the terminal, she pulled off the road into a view area, overlooking the shoreline of Lake Michigan. In the darkness and with snow falling, she could see the running lights of ferry boats shuttling passengers across the frigid water.

She was grateful on a night like this for the heat pouring into her car through the vents on the floor and dashboard. Sitting pensively in the driver's seat, with Daniel's letter beside her, she tuned into a radio station playing Christmas music.

Anne had married Daniel after graduating from college, and she had worked to support him as he earned his law degree. They lived separate lives while Daniel attended the University of Michigan, a day's drive from Milwaukee, and she worked at a friend's advertising agency.

Following graduation, they moved to California, where Daniel went to work for a studio. He fell in love with the beaches, the glamor of the movie industry, and the social life, which increasingly kept him away from home. Anne missed Milwaukee and never did take to the laid-back lifestyle out West. When she complained to Daniel about his never being home, they quarreled. After a year of his working for the studio and coming home late at night, suspicion gave way to anger.

Anne shook her head as the song "Baby, It's Cold Outside" began to play, causing her thoughts to drift back in time to the night Daniel had left her.

The breaking point came as she sat in the dark of their apartment, listening to the clock tick, and waiting yet another night for him to appear. As background noise, the radio played the sultry Christmas song.

She had just put their two-year-old son down for bed and gone back to the living room sofa to wait for Daniel. Anne had been doing that a lot—waiting for him to come home, wondering where he was and resenting his indifference to her concerns.

Finally, a key scratched in the lock and the back door creaked open. The scent of an unfamiliar perfume filled her senses as hot tears stung her eyes. Anne glared at Daniel accusingly. Like a kicked dog, his eyes fell to the floor, and she knew. How could he have been so reckless and stupid? How could she have been so clueless?

"Where have you been?" Anne asked him, though they both already knew the answer.

He continued staring down, and Anne noticed his scuffed and wet shoes. They'd tracked mud onto the carpet, leaving an ugly brown trail. If only this mess could be cleaned up as easily as a little mud.

"I don't know what to say," he finally mumbled.

"How long has it been going on?" Anne asked him, her tone flat.

Daniel glanced up from beneath dark eyebrows and pitifully said, "I don't know. A few months. It doesn't mean anything, though."

"It doesn't mean anything?! How can you say that?" Anne screamed back at him.

Angry tears escaped the corners of her eyes, and

she could feel the blood pumping through her chest. She wanted to slap him. "I don't know how to handle this," she screamed, her body now shaking. "We have a son! We're married. We promised to be faithful to one another! How can I ever trust you again?"

For several uncomfortable seconds, Daniel just looked at her through tears of his own. Finally he whimpered, "I need to go. I don't want to hurt you anymore. Maybe it's best we just get a divorce so you can find someone better than me."

With that, he turned and left, and her heart shattered the moment he shut the door. Hurt, betrayed, and rejected, she sobbed herself to sleep. In the morning, she was awakened by tiny fingers tugging at her hair. Spencer had gotten out of his little bed and was curled up behind her on the sofa.

"Go moning, Mommy!" Spencer whispered. "I wuv you dis much!" his arms stretched as far as he could reach before hugging her neck. Ever since he had learned to talk, this was their morning ritual. She hugged him back, not letting go for a long time.

"I'm hungwy," he finally said, and she got up to make his breakfast. Wearing a brave face, she decided to steel herself to the pain of Daniel's rejection. She still loved him, but she wouldn't share him with someone

else, especially if he didn't want to stay. It was time for her and Spencer to go home.

Getting her job back at the advertising agency in Milwaukee had been easy, and after a quick phone call to her old boss, she'd packed for herself and Spencer. A divorce had followed, and except for the details of sharing custody of Spencer, Anne and Daniel had taken up separate lives.

Three years after her move back to Milwaukee, Anne met Bryce at the bank where he worked as a teller. He took notice of her engaging smile each time she came in to deposit her paycheck. He finally worked up the nerve to invite her to dinner. She was guarded throughout the meal but couldn't help but notice the caring way he reacted when she told him about her son.

When Bryce had learned that Spencer played soccer, he'd been a faithful fan, showing up at Spencer's weekly games with oranges for all the kids. That really scored points with Spencer, not to mention Anne.

Bryce's kindness was the foundation of their friendship. Soon his attentiveness fostered her confidence in him as well. She had married Bryce because his thoughtfulness and love had helped her forget the pain of Daniel's betrayal. Now, even though it was something she dreaded doing, she was meeting Daniel at the airport so he could admit his mistake. Anne would be there for him, to offer support and to forgive him. That was what he needed, and a small piece of her needed it too.

Her thoughts were pulled back to the present as a police cruiser shot past her car, its siren wailing and lights flashing. She turned her head to follow the bright lights as the Christmas song that was playing on the radio was interrupted by a news report.

"A commercial flight from Denver crash-landed just minutes ago in Lake Michigan near Mitchell Airport," the announcer said. "Rescue personnel report that survivors have been pulled from the icy lake. At present it is unknown if there are any fatalities. Stay tuned for more details as they become available."

Her fingers shook as she punched Spencer's number into her phone. Answering, he said, "Hi, Mom."

"Hi, honey. Listen, the radio said a plane from Denver crashed in the lake. I'm worried because I still haven't heard from your father. Is there anything on TV?"

"Just a minute. I'll turn it on."

Anne turned toward the lake to watch the drama unfold less than a mile away. In the flood lights from several vessels, rescue crews were pulling bodies from the water. She couldn't tell which bodies were moving and which were lifeless.

"It was probably his flight," Spencer said numbly. "A lot of people seem to have made it off the plane, and he may be on one of the boats. I'm sure he's fine."

"I hope you're right, Spencer," she said. "Don't go anywhere until I get home. I love you. Please let Bryce know I'm still at the airport, waiting for Daniel."

She broke the connection and prayed that Daniel was safe as her eyes clouded over with tears and a sinking sensation hit her stomach.

ten

Shock and numbness engulfed Claire. Sitting aboard the ferry, wrapped in a heavy wool blanket, she stared out blankly across the black water. Everyone who had survived the crash was now safely aboard a rescue boat. The few people who were treading water had been recovered. But she still had not seen Daniel.

From the deck of the ferry, Claire could not remove her eyes from the plane as it slowly sank deeper into the water until it was gone. She overheard a crew member say that 147 people had made it off the plane safely. *That means thirteen are gone*, she thought sadly. She hoped that Daniel had somehow made it, but she feared the worst.

Nearby, the man who had been working with

Daniel was sobbing. Instinctively, Claire moved closer to him, putting an arm around his shoulder.

"It'll be okay," she softly reassured.

Looking into her eyes, he blurted, "Maybe for us, but one guy didn't make it out. He was helping a little boy. I got the kid out of there, but he was still trapped inside as my life boat floated away."

Life seemed to stop as Claire's heart skipped a beat. A lump in her throat grew bigger as she choked on her tears. The flooded plane had become Daniel's sinking grave. She wrapped her arms around the man, and they cried together.

The ferry docked and paramedics escorted those who were injured to St. Luke's South Shore Hospital, where police and airline officials questioned the survivors. The media waited hungrily along the lake shore and had set up their cameras to capture exclusive first reactions from the survivors. A police barricade offered space for emergency personnel to work and as much privacy as possible for the people who had just endured the crash. Claire watched as a police officer faced a bank of camera lights and spoke to reporters.

"Definitive information as to why the plane crashed won't be available until the National Transportation Safety Board examines the wreckage and the black boxes are recovered," he said. "However, early reports from the crew indicate that there was icing beneath the wind flaps, which caused the plane to stall. We are not certain at this point how it came to be so far off course, but blizzard conditions may have blown it away from its intended flight path and toward the lake."

"Can you tell us if there were any casualties?" a reporter shouted, shoving his microphone into the official's face.

"I can't confirm a number at this time, but there were casualties and severe injuries, including broken bones and hypothermia," he replied. "That anyone survived is a miracle. People don't just walk away from something like this."

Claire felt like throwing up. Daniel was one of the casualties. She had seen frozen bodies in the water that drifted too far from the plane to be saved before rescue boats came. And yet, she was basically unharmed. Nothing made sense.

An airline official was writing the names of the survivors on a clipboard. Claire gave her name and contact information, declined the offer of hotel accommodations, and then, still wrapped in her blanket, walked to the street. Flagging a cab wasn't hard since people had come from all over the city to gawk at the survivors and get in on the excitement. It was a twenty-minute trip to the ProHealth Clinic that specialized in brain tumors. Her parents would be worried.

eleven

After a warm embrace with her mom and dad, the tears came—tears of gratitude for her safe arrival, tears of sadness for her father's condition, and tears of joy that they were together at last. Recounting her experience during the crash, she quickly reassured her parents that she was all right but needed to rest.

"It's okay, honey. We'll talk more in the morning," her mother comforted.

Exhausted and emotionally drained, Claire drifted off to sleep in the armchair in her father's room while her mother and father rested in adjoining hospital beds. She awoke to her cell phone vibrating around 7:00 AM. The words "Journal Sentinel" appeared on the caller ID. She wasn't going to talk to the media and didn't answer. But trying to get back to sleep in the awkward arm-chair was impossible. She stood up to stretch and turn on the television, which she watched with interest.

The airline's CEO was making a statement at a news conference: "This is a tragic Christmas Eve morning, a day no one will soon forget," he soberly began. His eyes were bloodshot, and he looked as though he hadn't had any sleep. "Unfortunately, this flight had everything going against it with the changing temperatures, snow and ice, and late departure." He went on to say that it was too soon to speculate about the cause of the accident until after the NTSB had completed its investigation, which would depend on recovering the airliner from the lake.

He continued, "Eyewitness accounts report the plane made a relatively smooth landing on the water." Then he added, in defense of the pilot, "It is impossible, even for a superb pilot, to recover from stalls caused by excessive icing. Airliners are designed so they can be ditched and float in water. However, in this case, the aircraft filled quickly with water, an indication that there was probably a fracture in the fuselage. We won't know for sure until we can get a closer look at that plane . . ."

A spokesperson for the police department said several people had suffered injuries because they did not keep their heads low on impact and were struck by flying debris. Others were being treated for broken limbs and hypothermia.

By now Claire's parents were awake and also staring at the television. "This is such a tragedy, and so close to Christmas," her mom said sadly.

"I'm just glad you're safe, Claire," her dad added.

Claire was still numb, her emotions not yet responding. Her phone rang again, and again the caller ID said "Journal Sentinel." The newspaper had already called her twice, and it wasn't even 8:00 AM. She didn't want to talk to the media. Her main focus was to find Anne and Spencer—to finish what Daniel had begun.

She left the room to call Spencer. The cocktail napkin had remained wadded in her pocket, and she carefully opened it up and smoothed out its wrinkles. The ink was smeared, but she could still make out the numbers. Holding the crimson stone in her hand, she punched in the number.

What was she supposed to say? How are you supposed to tell someone his father is dead? She was
the last person Daniel had opened up to. Claire
knew she needed to share Daniel's remorse with
his family, but this was such an awkward situa-
tion. Now she would not only be the bearer of
bad news but the one to communicate his final
moments, to show them his heart. Still, she owed
Daniel that much—especially since he saved so
many lives, giving his own.

A raspy voice choked out, "Hello?"

"Is this Spencer?" Claire asked.

"Yeah, who is this?"

"My name is Claire; I need to speak to you
about your father."

"He's dead," Spencer replied hollowly. "Someone from the airline called a few hours ago, and
we're *not* talking to any reporters."

"No, wait, please. I have something to tell you
about him," she fumbled. "I was there. I saw the
whole thing. I want to talk to you about Daniel
and—"

He interrupted, "What could you possibly
tell me about him that I don't already know?
I'm sure you really *were there*, along with a

bunch of other reporters, but like I already told you, we're not talking to the media."

The line went dead. Numbly, Claire stared at her phone. Holding the rock in her hand, she squeezed it, trying to pull out whatever magic was left. Remembering how Daniel had originally acquired the rock, she thought she might have to throw it at Spencer to get his attention but quickly dismissed her anger. She would call again later, and, for now, try to enjoy Christmas Eve as best she could with her parents.

Claire was still wearing the clothes from the plane and needed to buy some things to replace what had been lost in the crash, so a few hours later, she and her mother left her father to watch TV while they did some shopping.

Familiar brick buildings and streets from her childhood popped into view as they drove to the shopping district. Strings of lights, red ribbons, and pine garlands were strung from the top of one lamp pole to the next. The night's snowstorm had left the city with wet sidewalks and snow piled alongside building walls and gutters. They saw a man dressed as Santa ringing a brass bell beside a Salvation Army kettle.

It was strange being in the mall. It was Christmas Eve, and though the news of the crash was everywhere, people were going about their business, hurrying to get last-minute gifts. Except for those who had lost loved ones in the tragedy, the holiday bustle was going on much as usual.

"Oh, Claire, we're so happy you're here," her mother gushed as they were driving back to the hospital. "We've missed you, and you certainly lifted your father's spirits. He looked so much better today, don't you think?"

Claire smiled but didn't reply. She hadn't seen her father for several years and didn't have any point of reference to judge a change in his appearance. To her, he looked pallid and sick. But his doctor had said he would be able to go home in the morning, just in time for Christmas, so that was good news.

When she finally spoke, Claire said, "Mom, I need to apologize. I've allowed my career to get in the way of our relationship. I should have made some trips home to see you and I feel so awful that I wasn't available for you to visit me in Colorado. Now Daddy is sick and . . ." Her words failed her as she began to cry. Then, in a voice choked with emotion, she added, "I haven't been a very good daughter. . . . I'm sorry."

Her mother was crying also, but she smiled as she put her hand on Claire's arm and said, "We would have loved seeing more of you, but we know you have important things to do. I'm just glad you'll be staying with us a few weeks." She managed a little chuckle as she added, "Just don't let four years and a plane crash happen again before the next time you visit."

Her mother's little joke relieved the heavy emotion of the moment, and they both laughed. It felt good.

"I'll be sure I don't," Claire promised. "In fact, I'm thinking about taking a break from work for a while to sort out my priorities. I've been thinking about making changes in my life for a while now."

"Well, whatever you decide, please keep your dad and me in the picture." Claire's mother paused before continuing, "We love you so much. It'd be great if you could be closer to us. We won't be around forever, you know."

Suddenly, Claire's phone chirped. Spencer's name showed on the caller ID.

"Hello?" she answered.

A voice very much like her mother's responded. "Yes, hello. I understand you called earlier this morning to talk to Spencer about Daniel."

"That's right," Claire replied. "I sat beside Daniel on the plane."

"Oh, my dear," Anne sighed. "I overheard the conversation and something about it just didn't feel right. Spencer told me it was a reporter, but I pressed him because it didn't add up. I couldn't stop thinking about how you wanted to tell him something 'about Daniel' and you said that you 'were there.' We're all heartsick and would appreciate knowing more about what exactly happened."

Remembering the night before, Claire's heart sank as she realized the obligation she felt to Daniel's family. Going to see them would interrupt the time she wanted to spend with her parents, but she hoped they would understand. Claire wrote down the address as Anne gave it over the phone, and they agreed to meet in the late afternoon on Christmas Day.

twelve

The house was decorated in red and gold lights, and a layer of snow covered the rooftop and yard. Claire cautiously traversed the slick walkway before ringing the doorbell. A tall, handsome man opened the door, and Claire recognized him from the photograph Daniel had shown her.

He reached to shake her hand and draw her into the entry hall of the house. "You must be Claire," he said. "I'm Spencer. Please come in."

As he offered to take her coat, he chuckled uneasily before saying, "Hey, I'm sorry about the phone call yesterday. I'd been fielding media calls all morning, and we just wanted to be left alone."

"Please, don't worry about it. I understand. I didn't want to talk to any reporters, either," she said, turning to look at his face and friendly blue eyes.

Spencer hung up her coat and led her into the living room, making small talk along the way. He said they had lived in this home since he was three. There was a swing set and sandbox in the backyard that had kept him busy. Claire noticed that the house was nicely furnished and well kept. Pictures of Spencer as a boy covered the walls, as well as photos from Anne and Bryce's wedding day.

Following Spencer through the kitchen, Claire smelled the fragrance of gingerbread and pine. An attractive couple in their mid-fifties sat on the sofa in a cozy room decorated for Christmas. The man stood and helped the woman to her feet.

"Hi, Claire," Anne said warmly as she stepped forward to embrace her. "Thank you for coming. I can't imagine how difficult this must be for you. Please tell us a little about yourself."

Two lounge chairs faced the couch, in front of a wood-burning fireplace. Spencer gestured for her to take a seat in one before he sat down in the other.

"I grew up in Milwaukee, but after high school I went to college and never really looked back. Because I work in Colorado, I was flying from Denver to spend Christmas with my parents. Daniel sat next to me on the plane. I can't imagine how hard this must be for you, and especially for Spencer to lose his father," Claire said respectfully.

She glanced at Spencer, who was slumped sadly in his chair. "Thank you," he said softly.

Three stockings hung from the fireplace beside a Christmas tree with bubble lights and shiny red ornament balls. A name was embroidered on each stocking.

Drawing a deep breath, Claire continued. "Even though I had just met Daniel, we immediately hit it off, and he told me about your . . . divorce and why he was coming here to Milwaukee." She hesitated, studying Anne's face and then looking at Spencer. "All he wanted to talk about was how much he loved you and how proud he was of you, Spencer."

Spencer sat with his head down and simply nodded.

Claire went on. "I hope this is okay to say, Bryce, but the other thing he told me was how sorry he was for walking out on Anne all those years ago. He was coming here so he could ask for your forgiveness, Anne—so he could have a fresh start."

The three of them sat quietly as Claire described the moments before and after the plane went down. Each shed silent tears, especially when she recounted Daniel's sacrifice to save the little boy.

"He called me before getting on the plane," Spencer said, his voice cracking. "I didn't know that would be the last time I'd ever hear his voice. But he said he loved me, and a few weeks ago he told me he was coming to apologize to Mom. He didn't have to hold onto that pain all those years."

Quiet moments of reflection ticked away. Then, getting up from the couch, Anne walked to the fireplace and picked up an envelope from the mantel. Holding it in her hand, she thought about what Daniel had written to her. She'd initially wondered how genuine he had been in his professions of sorrow and apology, but hearing those feelings from this young woman—a literal stranger—was proof of his sincerity. Twenty-five years had passed since Daniel's betrayal. Feeling Bryce's love every day had eventually healed her wounds, but Daniel had never had that, and she felt sorry for him in a way she could not have anticipated.

She knew how broken Daniel had become emotionally after their divorce. In some ways, her happiness and his misery had felt like just rewards, but deep down she'd wanted him to be happy too. Taking the letter out of its envelope, she gazed for a time at Daniel's handwriting.

"Of course I forgive you, Daniel," she whispered. "Now go and rest in peace." The letter settled onto the flames, curled slowly at the corners, and was then quickly consumed by the fire.

The living room glowed from the crackling fire and the lights on the tree. As part of a long-standing neighborhood tradition, Bryce and Anne left to go caroling with their friends. But sitting close to each other on the sofa, Spencer and Claire talked for hours. They swapped life stories until the sun had long since set.

They also talked more about the crash, and Spencer expressed his wonder over the fear Claire must have experienced as the plane was going down.

Claire responded, "You know, even though I had only just met your father, having him there next to me was a comfort. When I realized we were going down, he held my hand . . ." Tears sprang up in her eyes, and she had a hard time completing her thought. "I never realized how fragile life was until seeing how quickly it can be gone. This tragedy is changing my priorities—I want to live as best as I can, loving my family, friends, and myself."

They sat for a time, thinking about that, until Claire said, "Well, it's getting late. I should get home to be with my parents."

Spencer walked her to the front door and helped Claire with her coat.

"Would you mind if I called you sometime?" he blurted.

Buttoning her coat, Claire glanced at his face before looking into his eyes. "Sure," she said, smiling at him. "I'd like that."

Relieved, Spencer smiled back. "I need some time to take in all that's happened with Dad, but I'll call you soon."

Several days later Claire peeked into her father's study and knocked softly on the door. She saw her dad sitting behind a large oak desk that had once belonged to his father. When she was ten, Claire and her dad had restored the desk. They spent the summer sanding the wood drawers, handles, and tabletop surfaces. She could still remember the sound of her father's amused laugh as her nose curled from the fumes of an open can of wood stain.

"Hi, honey!" her dad called out warmly. Claire saw dozens of old photographs scattered across the desk.

"Hi, Dad. I just came to check on you to see how you're feeling today." More than a week had gone by since he was released from the hospital, and, like any family that endures a near death experience, Claire and her parents had spent most of the time sharing stories, staying close to each other, and caring for one another's needs.

"I'm feeling so much better now that you're here," he said, smiling. "Take a look at this picture. It's one of my favorites."

He held out a color photograph of a two-year-old girl carrying a blanket in one hand and holding her father's hand with the other. Their faces held matching expressions of smiling eyes and big grins.

"I know you don't remember this, but you couldn't find your blanket and cried your eyes out. All morning we looked everywhere. It wasn't until I thought to look in the kitchen cupboard where you liked to play that I saw it lying across the green beans. You were so happy that your mom hurried away to find the camera and take a picture."

Claire smiled at the way her father's eyes and spirit lit up as he told the story. He had spent his life taking care of her and making sure she had all the things she needed to make life more meaningful.

"I've really missed you, Dad," Claire said, falling into his arms. He stroked her hair and held her close like he had when she was a little girl.

"I'm glad you're home," he whispered.

Hangers full of discarded clothes littered the dressing room. Claire had a pile of clothing she wanted to buy, including jeans and blouses, but she still hadn't found anything to wear for her date with Spencer. He'd invited her to go ice skating at Red Arrow Park. If Claire ever did get her suitcase back from the airline, the contents would be unusable. Her mother passed another sweater over the door for Claire to try on.

"I think this one will look great on you," her mother gushed. "Plus it'll be warm beneath your coat."

Modeling the form-fitting, royal blue sweater, Claire opened the door and spun in a quick circle. "It really brings out your eyes and is so flattering," her mother said, smiling. "You'll definitely have to get this one."

Back at home, Claire spent several extra minutes in front of the mirror fixing her hair and makeup. She hadn't felt this much desire to look good for a date since college. As the doorbell rang, Claire accidentally smeared mascara on her eyebrow. She quickly rubbed it off and then skipped down the stairs. Her father beat her to the door by a few steps and gestured Spencer inside.

"Now you'll have her home by a decent hour, is that right, young man?" her father teased.

"Yessir," Spencer assured him. Then, seeing Claire, he said, "Strangely, I feel like I'm picking up my high school prom date." His smile was warm and his eyes intent. Claire noticed a little dimple beside his mouth when he laughed.

"Are you ready to go?" he asked, taking in the way she looked in her blue sweater. He felt like the luckiest guy on the planet, if only to be spending an afternoon with her.

"Well, you kids have fun. I'm going to take a nap in my new recliner," her father said, shuffling toward the family room.

Their breaths formed fluffy clouds as they made their way down the front walk. Spencer opened the passenger door for Claire, and she slipped into the seat.

Just breathe, Spence. Play it cool, he coached himself while walking around to the driver's side of the car. His pep talk did little to slow his heartbeat as he opened his own door and found her smiling at him. "What kind of music do you listen to?" he asked anxiously. Sensing his nervousness, she put a hand on his arm to calm him. That didn't help.

Inclining her head, she said, "I'm really into punk rock." Taken aback, he wrinkled his brow and cocked an eyebrow. He had totally misread her, thinking she'd be into something a little more sophisticated.

She laughed at his reaction and said, "I'm just kidding. I like country, but mostly I listen to classical music. I love following the composer on his musical journey."

"That's good," he said, relieved. "I'm a country fan myself. What's on your playlist?"

The outdoor ice rink was lined with trees that were fitted with strings of white lights. Happy faces were everywhere as they pulled up to the curb. Spencer opened Claire's door and was pleased when she took his arm to traverse the slippery path. They rented skates and walked over to the benches to put them on.

Bending down to tie her laces, she looked up at him over her shoulder and smiled. "Beat you to the ice!"

Surprising her, he jumped the wall and grinned. Then he said, "Hurry up, slow poke!"

A little rusty on skates, the couple made a few laps, teasing each other as both took ungainly spills. After one particularly bad tumble, Spencer said, only half joking, "Maybe it's time to get hot chocolate." Claire laughed and grabbed his hand, pulling him toward the center of the rink. "Don't be a quitter," she scolded.

The inviting glow from the Christmas lights surrounded them. They made another attempt to skate gracefully, holding hands, and trying to get into a rhythm. But Claire caught an edge and would have fallen if Spencer hadn't pulled her into an embrace.

Her face was raised, and, on impulse, he leaned down to kiss her. They each experienced a thrill as she snuggled into him, enjoying the warmth of his closeness. He felt a momentary dizziness as they held the kiss.

Finally pulling away from him, Claire smiled and whispered, "It's been a long time since I've done that." Spencer responded by holding her close. Every other thought had left his mind. He only wanted to be with her. Knowing they needed to talk, Spencer led her to a nearby bench, and they sat down facing each other. He touched her cheek and said, "I really want to see you again."

She turned her head away, forcing him to drop his hand. "Maybe we should slow things down," she said haltingly. "I don't know if it's right to jump into a relationship, given all that's happened. We don't even live in the same state."

The excitement of the moment caused her to begin shivering, and Claire put her hands in her pockets where she found the crimson stone. She pulled the stone from its warm place and showed it to Spencer.

"I almost forgot this," she said. "Daniel would have wanted you to have it. He believed the stone was magic."

Spencer took the stone from her and studied it. "As a teenager, when I spent summers with my dad, he'd often drag me to his office, where we could be together while he worked. I remember him showing me this stone. He said it held special powers, and I believed him because every moment I shared with him after seeing it that first time, he seemed to laugh deeper and his stories were funnier."

Spencer touched Claire's cheek again with his hand. He knew he had to balance her fear of moving too fast with his own desire to be close to her. He needed to convince her it was okay to jump into something new together. To earn her trust, he would have to take a chance and show Claire a part of his soul he'd never shown anyone.

"Look, I know we only just met, and I don't want to mess this up, but I've never met anyone like you before," he began. "I've been out with enough women to know you're someone special, and I want to give this my all and see where it might go. Seeing how much Dad hurt Mom, I decided a long time ago to never walk out on a relationship."

Claire looked up into Spencer's eyes. She couldn't deny that she had definite feelings for him, and she sensed he was being sincere.

"Maybe you're right. Maybe we need to just keep seeing each other to find out where this will lead," Claire agreed.

As Spencer reached for her hand, the stone accidentally fell into the snow. They both stared at the hole it made as it disappeared from sight. Giving a little cry of disappointment, Spencer reached down to retrieve it and then straightened and squeezed the stone tightly, remembering his father. He was grateful for Daniel's life and for his determination to correct his mistakes.

"This is something we should definitely hold on to," he said, smiling at Claire. "Maybe there's still a little magic left in it after all."

discussion questions

- The stone represented many symbols in the book. What are some of the stones you carry? Should you let them go?

- Some people use work as a distraction from forming healthy relationships. How would you help those who struggle with this?

- What responsibility do children have to their parents, particularly as they get older?

- Did Daniel make the right decision to try to apologize to Anne face-to-face?

- Anne showed tremendous resilience under the duress of Daniel's choices. Did she make the right decision by leaving him?

- How should you respond to life's tragedies?

- Why do you think Anne was able to forgive Daniel?

- Five years down the road, what do you think Spencer and Claire will be up to?

- Whose stone do you need to carry?

acknowledgments

Writing a book is never an easy venture, but it feels darn good when it's all wrapped up and ready for you, the reader, to bring the story to life. I owe a debt of gratitude to many different people who influenced this book, including Sara A. and Tammy P. for their help during a critical brainstorm after my initial outline was complete.

I'm very grateful for the insight and opinion shared by each of my pre-publication readers: Laura C., Eileen C., Colleen W., Summer M., Larry C., Sheralyn P., Elizabeth D., Alisha J., Kathy C., Brett S., Richard P., Mike C., and little Miss Ella C. A huge thank you to my sister Kathy for the wonderful sketches shown throughout the book— I hope you enjoyed Disneyland, even though Space Mountain broke down and the lights came on.

Many thanks are in order for the Cedar Fort team, especially those involved directly with the book, including Lyle M., Angie and Nate H., Jennifer F., Shersta G., Tanya Q., and Heidi D. A big thank you to Kenny H. for making the audio version a reality.

Recently I've seen several heart-breaking stories about families in crisis on the nightly news. Like so many others, I want to reach out and help those who are hurting. I'm grateful for the fine people at Primary Children's Medical Center and the healing work they do every day. It is a blessing to be able to play a small role in assisting their efforts by donating the author royalties from sales of this book.

The essential message of *The Christmas Stone* is one of neighbors helping neighbors. I hope the book encourages you to look for ways to lift the heavy stones your neighbors carry and to remember the journey with gratitude.

If *The Christmas Stone* inspires you to do more, here are suggestions for how to help:

1. Visit www.LizCarlston.com to find more information, book reviews, events, and giving ideas.

2. Suggest *The Christmas Stone* to a friend,

book club, colleague, church, woman's group, university or high school class, or a civic group.

3. Look for *The Christmas Stone* in your local library. If it isn't there, either donate a book or suggest to the library that they add *The Christmas Stone* to their collection. Ask friends or family in other states to do this too.

4. Encourage your local independent or chain bookstore to carry this book.

5. Write a review for *The Christmas Stone* at Amazon.com, Barnes & Noble, Borders, or a blog. Your opinion and comments help create additional awareness for this book.

6. Ask the arts and entertainment editor of your local newspaper or a producer at your favorite radio station to consider reviewing the book.

7. You might be surprised to learn that the families of one out of nine children who walk in the doors of Primary Children's Medical Center cannot afford to pay for their child's medical costs. If you want to support

these children in need, you can make a tax-deductible contribution to:

Primary Children's Medical Center Foundation
100 North Mario Capecchi Drive
P.O. Box 58249
Salt Lake City, UT 84158-0249

You can also donate by phone at (801) 662-5959 or online.

8. Please direct media inquiries regarding *The Christmas Stone* to liz.carlston@gmail.com.

about the author

Liz Carlston grew up in Littleton, Colorado. She has lived in Oakland and Palo Alto, California, and currently resides in Salt Lake City, Utah.

She is the author of two books, *Surviving Columbine* (2004) and *The Christmas Stone* (2010). Liz has appeared on CNN, ESPN, *Good Morning America* as well as in the *New York Times* and *Wall Street Journal*. Most recently, she has written articles for *The Daily Utah Chronicle* and

New Era magazine. She has also been spotlighted in the New York Times bestselling books *Columbine* by Dave Cullen (pp. 38–39) and *Fablehaven: Grip of the Shadow Plague* (pp. 417–18, 446, 454) by Brandon Mull.

All author royalties from *The Christmas Stone* (audio and paperback) will be donated to Primary Children's Medical Center.

To learn more or to contact the author, visit www.LizCarlston.com

0 26575 54341 4